MARVEL STUDIOS

CAPTAIN AMERICA™

THE FIRST AVENGER

MARVEL STUDIOS

CAPTAIN AMERICA

THE FIRST AVENGER

Adapted by Elizabeth Rudnick

Based on the Motion Picture Screenplay by Christopher Markus & Stephen McFeely

MARVEL

NEW YORK

MARVEL

Published by Marvel Press, an imprint of Disney Book Group. No part of this book may be reproduced or transmitted in any form or by any means, electronic or mechanical, including photocopying, recording, or by any information storage and retrieval system, without written permission from the publisher. For information address Marvel Press, 114 Fifth Avenue, New York, New York 10011-5690.

Printed in the United States of America

First Edition

3 5 7 9 10 8 6 4 2

J689-1817-1-11194

ISBN 978-1-4231-4306-2

MARVEL STUDIOS

CAPTAIN AMERICA™

THE FIRST AVENGER

CHAPTER ONE

Steve Rogers stood nervously in line at the army recruitment center in Bayonne, New Jersey. Ahead of him, men stepped up one by one. And one by one, they got approved to join the army. Steve sighed and waited for his turn, which seemed as if it would never come. Looking around, he noticed several newspaper headlines about a brutal attack on a small Norwegian town that had left civilians hurt and homeless.

America was at war. Across the ocean, Europe was full of gunfire and explosions. Men, women, and children were losing their lives and their homes as enemy forces invaded country after country. It had been going on for years before America got involved, but now soldiers from the

United States were flooding Europe, hoping to help the good guys win. But it wasn't going to be an easy—or a short—fight.

Steve felt the now-familiar rush of anger—and frustration. He wanted to be over there fighting more than anything in the world. But try as he might, he couldn't get past anyone in the recruitment centers, no matter how many attempts he made.

Steve had never been a big guy. Growing up on the streets of Brooklyn, New York, he and his best friend, James "Bucky" Barnes, had gotten into their fair share of fights. But it was usually Bucky who managed to keep them safe. Steve was scrappy, with small muscles, frail bones, and a list of ailments that made doctors roll their eyes.

Still, Steve had a big heart. And he figured that some army recruitment center would eventually give him what he wanted most—a 1A stamp. Then he could be an official United States soldier. Which is why he now stood in line in the fifth recruitment center in the fifth city, hoping this would be the day. He knew it was not exactly legal to try to enlist in multiple locations, but so far, no one seemed to have caught on.

"Rogers, Steven?" a voice called out, startling Steve.

He stepped forward, wiping his hands nervously on his pants.

The doctor opened his file and began to scan it, his eyes growing wide as he took in all the ailments that had been checked off. The paper looked like it had been attacked by a red pen. "Sorry, son," he said, looking up at Steve. "You'd be ineligible on your asthma alone."

He didn't say it, but Steve knew what he was thinking. *You're a fool, kid. The war is for strong men. Not for guys like you. Not for guys who can't even breathe right.*

"You can't do anything?" Steve asked anyway, hope in his voice.

"I'm doing it," the doctor answered. "I'm saving your life."

Then, as Steve watched, the doctor pulled

out the dreaded stamp. With a resounding thunk, he pressed it down on the file, marking it with a big, black 4F.

Steve had failed—again.

***

A short while later, Steve was back in Brooklyn, inside a darkened movie theater. Up on the screen, images from the front lines flashed by in a newsreel. There was a picture of a bombed-out town, followed by images of soldiers pulling wounded men out of the line of fire. Another image showed the enemy marching into an undefended town, knocking down people and buildings as they went.

Nearby, Steve heard the unmistakable sound of someone crying. So many people had already lost loved ones or were about to send them off to the front lines. Steve didn't have anybody who would miss him if he went. His parents had both died when he was young, and his closest friend, Bucky, had already enlisted and was being shipped off the next day. He would be over in Europe in no time, helping the army win the war, while Steve stayed behind, useless.

The sound of an angry voice broke through Steve's thoughts. "Jeez, play the cartoon already!" someone shouted from behind him.

Steve's eyes narrowed. What kind of guy would say something like that at a time like this? He turned in his seat and tried to see who had spoken, but the screen had gone dark for a moment and it was difficult to make out anyone in the shadows. "Can you keep it down, please?" he asked quietly, hoping that the person with the bad attitude would hear him.

But apparently he didn't because a moment later the guy called out, "Let 'em clean up their own mess!"

Steve shot out of his seat. He had had enough. "You want to shut up, pal?" he asked, turning. Then Steve's eyes grew wide. In the light of the screen, he could now see who was talking. The guy was huge, and he looked way too eager to fight.

Steve gulped. What had he gotten himself into?

In the alley behind the theater, Steve stood with his fists in front of him. Balancing on the balls of his feet, he bobbed and weaved from side to side, trying to look tough. But the other guy was easily double his size, with fists the size of Steve's head.

The big guy advanced toward Steve, who leaped forward, hitting him with an uppercut and then getting a good punch into his kidney. The hit made the man flinch—but only for a moment. He came back at Steve, swinging his meaty fists. Steve ducked one punch and then another. He stepped lightly back and out of the way as the guy swung again. Smiling, Steve tried to get another hit in.

But then his luck ran out. He tried to punch the guy but got too close, and in one quick move, the big man picked Steve up as though he were a rag doll and held him high above his head. His small, beady eyes narrowed, and then he slammed Steve down onto the hard pavement.

Struggling to get back the wind that had been knocked out of him, Steve unsteadily got to his feet. He shook his head, trying to clear his now-spotty vision. Then he grabbed the closest thing he found—a garbage-can lid—and held it in front of him like a shield.

The guy let out a mean laugh and then knocked Steve down yet again. He made a fist, pulled back his arm, and aimed for Steve's face. Just as he went to swing, someone grabbed his bicep, stopping him and momentarily saving Steve.

"What's with all the fighting?" a voice asked. "Don't you know there's a war on?"

Steve opened his eyes, which he had shut in anticipation of the punch, and smiled. He knew that voice. Bucky had arrived. He was dressed in his spotless uniform, a grin on his face as he took in Steve and the big guy. It wasn't the first time he had bailed out his best friend. With a swift kick, Bucky sent the other guy running out of the alley.

Making his way over to Steve, Bucky helped him to his feet. Then he reached down to pick up the jacket Steve had dropped when the fighting began. As he did, Bucky noticed a small piece of paper sticking out of the pocket. Pulling it out, he stifled a groan. It was another recruitment slip. He knew how much his friend wanted to be a soldier, but he also knew that it was probably not going to happen. And while Bucky would never say anything out loud, it sort of made him mad. True, he wanted to help his country win the war. But he was going to be shipped out tomorrow, and he was nervous. He didn't know what to expect across the ocean, and a part of him wished he had the same excuse Steve did.

Sighing, he handed the slip of paper back to Steve. "Tell me you didn't try to enlist again?" he asked.

Steve shrugged. "My day will come, Bucky," he said, his voice full of determination. Bucky couldn't possibly understand what it was like to be him. Even now, standing in the dirty alley, Bucky looked like a hero—something Steve could never be.

Seeing the sadness in Steve's eyes, Bucky decided to drop the subject. Time was precious now, and it seemed silly to waste it being in a bad mood. He had another idea. Holding up a newspaper, he smiled. On the front page was a picture of the fairgrounds with a title that read: 1942 WORLD EXHIBITION OF TOMORROW.

"Wanna go?" he asked.

Steve raised a curious eyebrow. Bucky wanted to go to a fair? Now? Shrugging, he followed his friend out of the alley. Maybe going to see an exhibition about "tomorrow" would help him forget all about today.

CHAPTER TWO

A few hours later, Bucky and Steve made their way onto the fairgrounds. At some point, Bucky had managed to find two young ladies to accompany them and was busy trying to get Steve to talk with one of them. But it wasn't working. Steve was too busy taking in the sights, particularly the Modern Marvels pavilion.

The fairgrounds looked like something out of a science-fiction novel. Huge, futuristic buildings had been erected, and they stood alongside smaller tents and pavilions. High above the ground, a monorail silently glided by, carrying passengers from one end of the exposition to the other. People of all ages wandered around, their eyes wide open at the various sights. Steve had to admit it was pretty amazing.

Making their way further into the fair, Steve and Bucky noticed a commotion over to one side. Walking closer, they saw a big sign that read: STARK INDUSTRIES. Standing on a raised platform next to a 1942 Cadillac was a man Steve recognized from the papers—Howard Stark. He was a millionaire inventor and notorious playboy who was always photographed out on the town with a beautiful woman on his arm.

As they watched, Stark smiled and pulled a lever. Suddenly, thanks to Stark's gravatic-reversion technology, the Cadillac lifted up off the ground. It was floating! The audience *oohed* and *aahed*, taking in the sight of the car of tomorrow. But then, with a thud, the car dropped back to the ground, shaking the platform. Stark just smiled again and began talking about how not even he was perfect.

Turning to say something to Steve, Bucky noticed that his friend was no longer by his side.

Even Steve's date didn't know where he had gone. Sighing, Bucky went to look for him.

He found Steve standing in front of the one nonfuturistic pavilion in the entire fair, the US Army recruitment pavilion. It looked empty. No one wanted to think about the war now, not when they could think about all the amazing things the future held. No one but Steve Rogers. He stood staring at the tent, enraptured.

"You're really going to do this now?" Bucky asked, walking over to stand next to him.

"I'm going to try my luck," Steve said, nodding.

"As who?" Bucky said, his voice harsh. "'Steve from Ohio'? They'll catch you, or worse, they'll actually take you."

That was it. Bucky had had enough. He was leaving for England tomorrow, and his best friend in the world wouldn't take the night off to have some fun with him, talk with some pretty girls, and maybe have a dance or two.

It was the first time Bucky had ever voiced his fears about Steve fighting in the war. Steve was taken aback by his friend's honesty.

"This isn't a back-alley scrap, Steve," Bucky continued, his voice softening. "It's a war."

"No," Steve corrected. "It's *the* war. The war we can't lose. This is the one that counts—and I mean to be counted."

Steve took a step toward the tent, and Bucky put a hand on his arm. "Come on," he said. "It's my last night."

His friend turned and gave him a wry smile. There was nothing Bucky could say or do that would convince Steve to leave that pavilion. Holding out his hand, he and Steve shook. It was time to say good-bye.

Bucky watched his friend go, his heart heavy. He hoped, for Steve's sake, that he would get what he wanted. He just wasn't convinced that when Steve got it, it would make him happy.

There was a part of Steve that knew he was being ridiculous. How many more times could he fail? And it was Bucky's last night. But if there was even the slimmest chance that his luck could change, then he had to take it.

Walking inside the recruitment center, his eyes quickly adjusted to the dark. Where outside it was all bright lights and noisy crowds, inside it was quiet and somber. Out of the corner of his eye, Steve saw an older man. He looked tired, as though being there took all of his energy.

The man made his way slowly over to Steve. "So, you want to be a fighter, heh?" he asked in a German accent.

Steve was momentarily taken aback. He hadn't expected a German national to be inside a US Army recruitment center. "You're with the army?" he asked hesitantly.

"Doctor Abraham Erskine," the man said, nodding. "Special Scientific Reserve, US Army."

Steve had never heard of the Special Scientific

Reserve but figured there were a lot of things he hadn't heard of. Shrugging, he gave Erskine his name and looked on as the man found his file. Steve tried not to grimace when he once again saw all the red x's, marking each and every one of his ailments and weaknesses.

Erskine finished reviewing the file and then looked up. "Five exams in five tries in five different cities," he said. "All failed. You are very tenacious, yes?"

How did he know that? Steve wondered. He thought that by going to different cities, he would have stayed under the radar and that the army wouldn't see how desperate he was to enlist. Maybe this Special Scientific Reserve, whatever it was, had more intel than the other branches of the army.

Outside, a pair of men wandered by and turned when they heard Erskine's European accent. They took a step forward as though to do something when Steve held up a warning hand.

Figuring it wasn't worth it, they moved on.

"A fella has to stand up," Steve said, turning back to Erskine. "I don't like bullies, Doc. I don't care where they're from."

The old man nodded thoughtfully. "So you would fight, yes," he said. "But you are weak and you are very small."

Steve was about to protest when Doctor Erskine did something unexpected: he laid out Steve's file on the table and picked up a stamp. Steve's heart began to beat faster.

"I can offer you a chance," Doctor Erskine said. "Only a chance."

Then, as Steve watched with growing excitement, the man pressed the stamp down on the file. Holding up the file, Steve saw a big 1A.

He couldn't believe it. After all this time, he was actually in the army. His luck *had* changed. Just like he told Bucky it would.

As Erskine began talking about next steps, Steve tried to pay attention. But his mind was spinning. He had no idea what kind of group the SSR was or why they would okay someone like him. Should he be worried? Was Bucky right when he said the biggest danger would come if someone *did* let him in? What if this was all some sort of joke? Maybe when he got outside he'd see Bucky laughing, having pulled a fast one on his old friend.

Shaking off those thoughts, Steve focused on Erskine. Whatever the SSR was and whatever the reason they had for taking him, Steve didn't care. He was in. Soon, he would be a real soldier, and maybe, someday, he'd even be an American hero.

CHAPTER THREE

Steve Rogers wasn't the only one chosen by the Special Scientific Reserve. A few days later he found himself standing in line at Camp Lehigh in the practice field with eleven other recruits. They were all healthy and tall and strong, and next to them, Steve felt even smaller than he usually did. But that didn't stop him from signing the last-will-and-testament document without a moment's hesitation. While the other recruits were all nervous about signing their lives away, Steve was willing to give all that he could to the US Army, even if it meant his own life.

Steve and the rest of the recruits filed into a large room, where Steve spied a man and a woman, watching and waiting. The man scowled at Steve, who was relieved to see Doctor Erskine off to one side, observing the recruits. The other man then introduced himself as Colonel Chester Phillips. He stood ramrod straight, multiple medals shining on his uniform. Deep lines were etched on his face, marking the combat missions that he had survived. Yet his eyes were still bright, clear, and serious as they surveyed the room.

Colonel Phillips addressed the men: "The Strategic Scientific Reserve is an Allied effort, made up of the best minds in the free world," he began. With that, the colonel then introduced Doctor Erskine and Agent Peggy Carter, who was on loan to the army from British Intelligence, and, despite her obvious beauty, looked only slightly less intimidating than Colonel Phillips.

When Agent Carter began to speak, Steve noticed that there was a lot of quiet chuckling and chattering going on. The recruits kept eyeing Peggy, taking in her long legs and pretty face.

Walking over to a man by the name of Hodges, Peggy asked him if he knew judo. When he replied that he didn't, she executed a perfect judo move, grabbing his arm and twisting it back, hard. He yelped and dropped.

"Do you have anything else to say?" she asked. When he shook his head no, Peggy let him go and walked back to the front of the room. After that, the recruits paid her their full attention.

And it was a good thing they did, because the training started right away. First up was the obstacle course. As he stood waiting for his team's turn, Steve tried to remember everything he had read about obstacle courses. He knew that they were supposed to help a soldier learn how to handle combat situations while building a sense of team camaraderie. But looking out over the various objects on the course, and then taking in the men standing on either side of him, he doubted that would happen. The obstacles included a climbing wall, rope swings, a rappelling wall, a long piece of wood that looked like a balance beam but with a rough surface, large rubber tires, and even a deep mud puddle.

The men already on the course raced through the obstacles, easily climbing over the wall and nimbly running across the balance beam. It looked as if they had been doing this sort of thing their whole lives.

"Our goal is to create the finest army in history," Colonel Phillips said as they waited. "But every army starts with one man. By the end of this week, we're going to choose that man. He's going to be the first of a new breed of Super-Soldiers."

Super-Soldiers? Steve repeated silently. Was there something going on he didn't know about? But he didn't have time to think about it as a horn sounded, signaling his turn to go. He leaped at the wall, trying to pull himself over, but one of the other men's boots landed squarely on his head, pushing him back. By the time he made it over, he was way behind the others. He could see Phillips,

Peggy, and Erskine watching and increased his speed. But he knew that he'd already made a bad impression. He had to pick up his game.

Erskine turned to Phillips, his mind made up. "Rogers is the clear choice," he told the colonel. But Phillips couldn't disagree more.

"You put a needle in that guy's arm," the Colonel began, "it's going to come out the other side."

Phillips continued to watch Steve, who was once again the last in line. "Look at him," Phillips said to Erskine, "he's making me cry."

But the course continued, and so did Steve. He scrambled up a cargo net only to get tangled in it when Hodges walked over him. But he recovered and kept going. He crawled through mud covered by barbed wire only to have Hodges kick out a support beam, causing the barbed wire to fall on Steve. Still, he kept going.

His efforts didn't go unnoticed.

Agent Carter and Doctor Erskine had seen

Hodges try to sabotage Steve over and over again. And yet each time, Steve had gotten back up, more determined than ever. He didn't have the muscles of the other recruits, but he had something they didn't—heart. He would fight as hard as he could as long as he could and never turn a back on a fellow soldier. Those were the qualities Peggy and Erskine were looking for. Phillips, however, didn't feel the same way. He still saw Steve as a weak, ineffectual soldier-in-training.

Phillips wanted Hodges for the job and wasted no time in voicing his opinion. "He's big, he's fast, he takes orders. In short, he's a soldier."

"No," Erskine interrupted. "He's a bully."

Phillips immediately countered Erskine's argument. "You don't win wars with niceness, Doctor. You with them with guts." And to prove his point, Phillips picked up a grenade and hurled it into the middle of the course, right near Steve.

As Hodges and the other recruits panicked and fled, Steve ran right at the grenade. "Everybody down!" he shouted as he flung himself on top of the explosive device.

There was a moment of silence as everyone waited for the inevitable. One second passed. Two seconds. Three. Finally, Steve gingerly eased himself up and off the grenade. Looking over to where Phillips, Peggy, and Erskine stood, he cocked his head and asked, "Is this a test?"

Peggy tried not to smile. It was a test of sorts, and not even Colonel Phillips could deny that Steve had passed. The SSR didn't need to look any further: Steve Rogers was going to be their first Super-Soldier.

Later that night, Steve sat inside the now-empty barracks. The rest of the recruits had been sent home, and the empty beds made Steve feel oddly alone. But a part of him was excited about what the future held. Peggy and Doctor Erskine had given him more details once he was chosen; he was to be given a special serum that Erskine had created. With luck, it would turn him into a man with extraordinary powers. He'd be able to run faster, hit harder, and think quicker—all things that would be helpful on the battlefield. But there would also be risks undergoing such a procedure—namely, would he survive the experiment?

The sound of footsteps echoed in the empty room, and Steve looked up. Erskine had entered the barracks and was walking toward him. As always, the doctor's expression was somber.

"Can I ask you a question?" Steve said when the older man took a seat on the bed across from him. Erskine nodded. "Why me?"

The scientist smiled. He had been expecting this question. And Steve deserved to know the answer—and the history behind the serum.

Five years ago, Erskine began, he was living in Germany working as a scientist. His experiments were radical, and some felt they were foolish. But then he had invented a serum that had the possibility of giving a man almost-superhuman abilities. It promised great power to anyone who controlled it and, as the war was just beginning, the potential for whoever had it to be victorious. Erskine was eager to keep it out of the wrong hands—but then a man named Johann Schmidt found out about his discovery.

Schmidt, Erskine explained, was himself a brilliant scientist, and also the leader of an organization called HYDRA. At the time that Erskine worked with him, Schmidt was fascinated with occult powers and Teutonic myths. But Schmidt longed for his own glory, no matter what the cost. Schmidt believed that worlds existed in which men had the strength of gods and could control weather and the elements. He became obsessed with the idea that a great power had been hidden on Earth by the gods and was waiting to be seized by a superior man. Schmidt—and HYDRA—vowed to find that power.

Steve raised an eyebrow and Erskine nodded as if to say, yes, insane, I know. Then he continued.

Schmidt believed that Erskine's serum was the key to that power. And he wanted it. Despite Erskine's every attempt to stop him, Schmidt got his hands on the serum and, in an act of desperation, injected himself.

The results were horrific, and the experiment was a failure.

Erskine had no choice. He fled his country and made his way to the United States in the hope of keeping the rest of the serum out of Schmidt's hands. But he knew that the HYDRA leader would never stop looking for him—or the serum. The failed experiment had corrupted Schmidt, and in Erskine's eyes it had turned the scientist into a monster.

"This is why you were chosen," Erskine said to Steve, who had been listening intently. "A strong man, he might lose respect for power if he had it all his life. But a weak man knows the value of strength . . . and compassion."

The scientist sighed deeply. He saw the doubt in Steve's eyes and couldn't blame him. It was a rather unbelievable story. But it was an important one. For Erskine had learned a valuable lesson.

"The serum amplifies what is inside," he finished. "Good becomes great. Bad becomes worse." Erskine looked Steve straight in the eyes. "Whatever happens tomorrow," he said, "promise me you'll stay who you are. Not a perfect soldier, but a good man."

Steve nodded in silence. Tomorrow was going to be a very interesting day. He just hoped that Erskine and Peggy were right about him. He didn't want to think about what would happen if they were wrong.

CHAPTER FOUR

The next day Peggy picked up Steve early in the morning and took him away from Camp Lehigh. They soon found themselves driving through the streets of Brooklyn, New York. For the first time since the night of the exhibition, his thoughts drifted to Bucky and to their misspent youth on the means streets of Brooklyn.

"I know this neighborhood," Steve said proudly to Peggy. "I got beat up in that alley . . . and over there . . . and there."

Peggy looked at him quizzically. "Did you have something against running away?" she asked.

"You start running," Steve began, "they'll never let you stop. You stand up, you push back . . . they can only tell you no for so long, right?"

Peggy smiled to herself, more confident than ever that the SSR had made the right choice in picking Steve Rogers.

The car came to a stop, jolting Steve. Looking around, he saw that they had parked in front of an antiques store.

"Why did we stop here?" he asked, confused.

"I love a bargain," she answered simply, opening the car door and getting out. Steve laughed. Peggy was full of surprises, and he felt a weird flutter in his chest. He hated to admit it, but he was starting to like Peggy.

Getting out of the car, he followed her inside. An old woman stood behind the counter, surrounded by various knickknacks, and dusty antiques. With one hand on a machine gun, the woman nodded at Peggy, then pressed a hidden button, allowing Peggy and Steve to enter.

At a door in the back of the store, Peggy stopped and turned to make sure Steve was behind her. Then she opened the door, revealing a secret staircase. They made their way down and walked through another door—right into the Special Scientific Reserve Rebirth lab.

Steve's eyes grew wide as he took in the giant space. Far longer than the store above, it was illuminated by bright lights and bustling with activity. In the center of the ultramodern area, technicians operated different kinds of machinery, consulting with one another as they pulled levers and flipped switches. A group of engineers manned a row of monitors that beeped with information, while in another part of the lab a film crew was setting up their equipment.

Looking up, Steve noticed an observation booth. Several serious-looking men stood inside talking. Peggy quickly informed him that the man with the salt-and-pepper hair was Senator Brandt. He had helped the SSR get funding for the serum experiment—code-named Project: Rebirth—and was here to see if his money had been well spent.

As Steve walked further into the lab, everyone turned to stare at him. He smiled self-consciously when he realized that he might be in over his head. Instinctively, he made his way to Doctor Erskine, who stood next to a large cradlelike device that was shaped like a man. This, Erskine informed him, was the Rebirth device. It was in this cradle that Steve would be given the serum.

With a deep breath, Steve got inside. It was now or never.

"Comfortable?" Doctor Erskine asked.

At Steve's nod, Erskine smiled. Then, turning to the attendants standing at the ready, he gave them the signal. They began to hook up Steve to various wires, tubes, and monitors. These would help Erskine observe Steve's reactions as the experiment proceeded.

"How are your levels, Mr. Stark?" Erskine asked, turning to someone Steve hadn't noticed before.

The man turned and Steve raised an eyebrow.

It was Howard Stark, the inventor he had seen at the World Exhibition of Tomorrow. Stark wasn't a military man, so he must also be on loan to the SSR, Steve thought.

"Coils are at peak," Stark replied to Erskine. "Levels are one hundred percent. We're ready." Then he paused before adding, "As we'll ever be."

Erskine didn't seem as concerned. Picking up a microphone that would carry his words into the observation booth, he began to speak. "Today, we take the first step on the path to peace," he said. Behind him, more attendants fiddled with the machines hooked up to Steve. A heart monitor began to beep in time with Steve's racing heart.

"The serum will cause immediate cellular change," Erskine went on. "In order to prevent uncontrolled growth, the subject will then be saturated with vita rays."

Uncontrolled growth? Saturated with rays? The heart monitor started beeping faster as Steve listened. So his cradle was going to turn into a chamber? And he'd be shot full of rays? If Bucky were here right now, Steve thought, he'd tell me, "I told you so."

Turning off the microphone, Erskine nodded to a nurse. She opened up a case, revealing an aluminum syringe. She tapped it a few times, pulled back the plunger, and injected Steve in the arm.

"That wasn't so bad," Steve said when she was done.

"*That* was penicillin," Erskine said, a small smile on his face.

As Steve looked on, a panel slid back, revealing a carousel of blue vials. There were seven tubes of serum in total. Erskine and the nurse began inserting the vials one by one into the injectors set up around Steve. When they had inserted six of the seven, Erskine had another technician move closer. He was in charge of the injector pads—small round objects covered with hundreds of tiny needle tips. They were lightly placed all over the outside of Steve's body. When they were pressed down into his skin, the serum would flow through the injectors, into the pads, and then into Steve.

Steve was about to say something along the lines of, "Hold on, maybe we should wait a minute," when he was pressed back into the cradle.

Then Erskine began the countdown. "Beginning serum infusion in five, four, three, two . . . one."

He pressed a switch, and Steve jerked as the pads pressed down on him. The blue fluid flowed from the injectors. Instantly, Steve's veins began to swell and his head began to shake, as the fluid washed through him.

Erskine hit another button and padded restraints closed around Steve's head, calming the shaking. But it didn't stop his eyes from turning blue. From the look on Erskine's face, though, it seemed as if this was supposed to happen.

When the six vials were finally empty, Erskine turned to the millionaire inventor. "Now, Mr. Stark."

Stark pulled a lever, and the cradle began to tilt. When it was finished moving, Steve was straight up, and the cradle looked like a rocket ready to launch. Then a panel slid across the cradle, sealing Steve inside. Through a small window, everyone could see Steve's face, his eyes still glowing blue. With the panels closed, the cradle was now ready to be flooded with vita rays which would hopefully keep Steve safe. The vita-ray machine came courtesy of Howard Stark, who gave Steve a reassuring nod before moving to the control device.

A piercing whine filled the air as Stark turned a power dial. On a big gauge, a needle began to climb, indicating the level of rays flooding the chamber. It hit ten, then twenty. Steve's face began to tense. At forty, his eyes squeezed shut. Then the needle reached sixty, and the heart monitor began beeping wildly. The rays were affecting Steve badly. Stark looked to Erskine, ready to turn the machine off, but the scientist shook his head. They had to keep going.

The needle reached eighty, and a strange orange glow filled the device chamber. Steve's face could no longer be seen through the window. Inside, Steve was completely unaware of what was going on as the rays battered his body. Outside, Erskine's own heart pounded. He knew he was putting Steve in great danger, but he had to. . . .

When the needle hit ninety, Steve let out a piercing scream. Up in the booth, Brandt and his aides took a step back when they heard it. On the lab floor, Erksine watched as the orange light grew even brighter. It was too much. "Kill the reactors!" he ordered.

Stark was about to turn the dial down when over the microphone Steve's voice came, faint but determined. "No," he said. "I can do this."

Erskine swallowed. They had chosen Steve because he had heart, and it seemed he was determined to see this through. The doctor hesitated and then finally nodded at Stark. The other man gave the dial a final turn. One hundred. A sharp whine split the air, and the chamber flashed from orange to white.

Then everything went dark.

Silence filled the lab. The heart monitor stopped beeping and no sound came from inside the chamber. Up in the booth, Brandt looked down at Erskine, his expression a mixture of disappointment and anger. Everyone in the room held their breath in anticipation.

Then, suddenly, the heart monitor came to life. *Beep, beep, beep.*

Anxious, Erskine took a step forward. Had it worked? Was it possible?

There was only one way to tell. Stark opened the chamber.

Scientists peered through the smoke and machinery as the chamber cleared of the last rays. And then, Erskine smiled.

Steve was still strapped into the chamber. But it wasn't the same Steve who had gone in.

No longer was he thin and frail. Instead, he was now a model of human perfection, standing a foot taller than before with muscles rippling all over his new body. Project: Rebirth had worked!

"You did it, Doctor!" Stark shouted, as he unstrapped Steve, who was momentarily weakened from the ordeal. "You really did it!"

As Stark helped Steve over to a chair, everyone rushed in, eager to see the results and congratulate each another. In the middle of the excitement, Steve sat, taking everything in. He felt different. He couldn't tell what he looked like, but from the reactions of those around him he figured it was good. And from the reaction of Peggy, he figured it was *very* good. "How do you feel?" she asked.

"Taller," he said, looking down at her as he smiled.

Peggy smiled back. At least his spirits hadn't changed.

And then everything started to go downhill— fast.

While they were talking, one of the men who had been in the observation booth made his way into the lab. He wore glasses and went by the name Fred Clemson. Ignoring Doctor Erskine and the others, he made his way to the chamber—and the last remaining vial of serum. Glancing quickly around to make sure no one was looking, he pulled out a lighter. With a flick of his thumb, he opened it, revealing a button instead of the usual wick.

Erskine heard the sound through the chatter in the lab and turned. He knew that sound. His eyes grew wide. He also knew that person. His name wasn't Fred Clemson. His name was Kruger, and he was a HYDRA agent. Erskine saw Kruger at the same time the other man saw him. An evil smile spread across Kruger's face, and his thumb pressed down on the lighter. Then he threw it.

"No!" Erskine shouted. But it was too late. The room exploded.

CHAPTER FIVE

Everything was going according to HYDRA's plan. Kruger had infiltrated the Special Scientific Reserve's headquarters just as he'd been instructed. And he had destroyed their lab, just as he'd been told. Now he needed to get his hands on the last remaining vial of serum and make his escape.

Through the smoke, Kruger saw Erskine, who was still seen as a traitor by the HYDRA organization. Pulling out his pistol, Kruger aimed and fired. Erskine went down. Grabbing the vial, Kruger headed for the door.

Hearing the shot, Steve looked up. He was still shaky from the experiment—and the explosion—and his limbs felt out of sync with the rest of his body. But when Steve saw Erskine fall, he jumped to his feet and raced over to his friend. But it was too late. Erskine was mortally wounded. He managed to whisper the name "Kruger," and then his eyes closed.

For a moment, Steve didn't know what to do. Erskine was dead. The lab was in shambles. And a spy was racing off with the last vial of serum. How had everything gone from so good to so terribly bad in such a short amount of time? Shaking his head, Steve saw Kruger heading for the door. Kruger turned his gun on the old woman. She was reaching for her machine gun, but the HYDRA agent was faster. He made his way out of the antiques shop.

But Steve wasn't going to let him get away.

Jumping to his feet, he took off after the agent. When Steve burst out onto the street, he was just in time to see Kruger pulling the driver out of a taxicab. He threw the poor man to the ground and jumped into the cab. Peggy, who had chased after Kruger, pulled out a gun and opened fire. Kruger returned fire, hitting a car behind Peggy, causing it to explode into flames. Then, with a squeal of tires, Kruger peeled out and raced away.

Peggy thought the HYDRA spy would get away. Until she saw Steve.

Steve Rogers was now very fast. Superfast. He charged after Kruger, running as quickly as his new legs could carry him. Kruger drove down an alley, then turned and kept going, with Steve just a few feet behind. With a huge roar, Steve launched himself at the taxi, landing with a thud on the roof. Behind the glass, Kruger's eyes narrowed and he raised his arm. He still held his pistol. With a smile, he fired, shattering the cab's window. Steve ducked to the side. His grip loosened on the hood and he fell, clinging with all his might to the cab.

The buildings rushed by as Kruger drove on, heading toward the Brooklyn piers. Suddenly, up in front, Kruger saw a truck roaring toward him. He jerked the wheel, but it was too late. The truck sideswiped the cab, sending it—and Steve—into a roll. The world spun upside down as the cab flipped over and over again, finally coming to a stop, its hood smoking.

As Steve struggled to his feet, Kruger stumbled out of the wreckage, gun firing. Steve ducked, but the bullets were flying too fast. Thinking quickly, he grabbed a cab door that had been knocked loose and held it up in front of him like a shield. The bullets bounced off the metal, richoceting harmlessly. Kruger kept firing.

Their high-speed ride had taken them right down to the piers, which, on the sunny day, were filled with civilians catching the sights and enjoying the afternoon. Seeing the commotion, some of them began snapping pictures of the gunfight, mistaking it for entertainment. Then Kruger turned, shoving pedestrians aside as he ran.

Seeing a young boy among the gathering crowd, Kruger grabbed him and pulled him to his chest, holding the gun to his head. Steve slowed down as Kruger began moving backward toward the water. When he was close enough to jump, Kruger threw the boy into the water and pulled out a small device. He clicked a button and a small one-man submarine surfaced a few feet away. Kruger gave Steve an evil smile and then scrambled into the HYDRA sub.

Steve looked down at the water. He couldn't let Kruger get away, but he also couldn't let the little boy drown.

"Go get him!" the boy shouted, interrupting Steve's thoughts. "I can swim."

"Great," Steve muttered, more to himself than the kid. "I can't."

But he had no choice. The boy was okay and Kruger had to be stopped. Taking a deep breath, Steve ran to the edge of the pier and jumped, landing in the chilly water. The cold knocked the air out of Steve's lungs, and for a moment he wondered if he was going to drown in spite of his newfound superpowers. But then his legs began to kick on their own accord, and before he knew it he was slicing through the water with long, powerful strokes. In no time, he had caught up to the sub. Reaching out, he grabbed its tail fin. Pulling himself forward hand over hand, he made it to the cockpit. Through the glass, he saw Kruger's eyes widen at the sight of him. Then Steve pulled back his fist and punched the glass over and over again. With a mighty crack, it broke, allowing water to rush inside.

Reaching into the cockpit, Steve grabbed Kruger and yanked him free of the now-sinking sub. Then, with another mighty kick, he headed toward the surface.

Back on dry land, he threw Kruger to the ground. But the HYDRA soldier wouldn't give up. He pulled out a knife and tried to stab the American. Steve effortlessly kicked the knife aside. As he lunged at Kruger, the vial of blue serum dropped out of Kruger's hand, and into the water below.

"Who are you?" Steve yelled.

"The first of many," he said cryptically. Then, Kruger pressed his tongue against a false tooth, triggering a cyanide pill. "Cut off one head and two more shall take its place." His body began to shake and his mouth started to foam. Right before Kruger died, he said, "Hail HYDRA."

Steve sat there for a long time after Kruger died, his mind racing. What sort of organization would send someone like Kruger to kill Erskine and harm innocent people? And now that they had failed to get their hands on the serum, would they also come after Steve? A few seconds later, Peggy arrived with additional SSR men. Steve looked to Peggy for advice, but her words brought no solace.

"All of Doctor Erskine's research and equipment is gone. Any hope of reproducing the project is locked away in your genetic code." She put her hand on Steve's shoulder. "At the moment, you're the only Super-Soldier there is," she said.

CHAPTER SIX

Back at SSR headquarters, Colonel Phillips and Senator Brandt were in the middle of a heated discussion. Phillips paced back and forth, his expression furious. They had been attacked on their own soil by an enemy spy who had managed to sneak in with the senator's entourage. It was a disgrace. And now, on top of it, Erskine was dead, and with him any hope of creating more Super-Soldiers. If HYDRA had gotten their hands on that one vial . . . Phillips shivered at the thought. The SSR had only one option—go after HYDRA before they came back after them.

As Phillips paced, Steve entered the headquarters. He had changed into a clean set of clothes that actually fit, but he looked tired from the events of the past few days.

Seeing him, Phillips grew even angrier. "I asked for an army!" he fumed. "All I got is you. And you are *not* enough."

Steve's head dipped as shame rushed over him. He felt like a failure. Everyone had put their faith in him, and he hadn't been able to keep Kruger from killing Erskine or taking the cyanide pill.

While Phillips fumed, Senator Brandt remained silent. Whereas the colonel was a ball of nerves, Brandt seemed eerily calm. He wasn't convinced that the experiment had been a failure. As if to prove it, he held up a copy of the day's paper. "You've seen Steve here in action," he said. "But more importantly, the *country's* seen it."

Walking closer, Phillips looked at the headline. It read: MYSTERY MAN SAVES CIVILIANS! Below it, there was an image taken of Steve the day before on the piers. He was using the cab door as a shield while Kruger fired.

Brandt waved the paper. "You don't take a

soldier—a symbol—like this and hide him in a lab." Turning to Steve, he flashed his trademark smile, the one that had made him the successful senator he was. "Son, do you want to serve your country?" Steve nodded. "On the most important battlefield in this war?"

Of course Steve wanted to help. That was the whole reason he was in this situation in the first place. "It's all I want," he said.

The senator's smile got larger as he walked over and clapped Steve on the back. "Then congratulations. You just got promoted."

It didn't take long for Steve's promotion to go into effect. But it wasn't exactly what he'd been expecting.

A few days later, he found himself backstage in a small theater. His palms were sweaty, and he looked as if he was going to be sick to his stomach. One of Senator Brandt's aides stood next to him, running through what was about to happen. Steve barely heard him.

"I don't think I can do this," he said softly. When Brandt had promised him that he would get to take part in the greatest battle of all, he had pictured being on the front lines, battling the enemy and saving his fellow soldiers. Not standing behind a curtain on a stage, preparing to do a song-and-dance act. But that was exactly what he was doing.

Before Steve could get any more nervous, the show began. The curtains parted, and a bugler walked onto the stage. He tilted his head back and blasted out reveille. Then, as the final notes faded, a band joined in and line of girls danced across the stage, legs kicking high in the air. As Steve watched with a mixture of horror and embarrassment, they began to sing: "He's the star-spangled man with the star-spangled plan. He's Captain America!"

As they sang out the last word, Steve took a deep breath and moved forward. The aide had told him what to do. He was supposed to just walk through the flag and say his lines to the audience. But he felt like a fool. He was dressed in what Senator Brandt had decided made him look most like "Captain America"—the war's newest hero—red boots and gloves, a pair of blue pants, and a shirt covered with stars and stripes. To top off the look, he had been given a mask with wings and a cheap red, white, and blue shield. Steve had refused to look in the mirror, but he was mortified anyway. How was he supposed to inspire people to support the war looking like a kid in a Halloween costume? And what if the audience realized he'd never even set foot on the front line?

A shove from the aide reminded Steve that he hadn't moved. He stumbled forward past the flag and saw just a handful of kids sitting in the audience. So much for the big crowd Brandt had promised, Steve thought. Taking a deep breath, he eyed the cue card he had pasted on the back of his shield and began to speak. "Hello . . . uh, folks," he said. "Who here is ready to sock evil on the jaw?"

The kids let out a cheer, and Steve felt his shoulders relax. Maybe this wouldn't be so bad after all.

For the next few months, Steve traveled all over the United States performing his Captain America show. At first, the crowds were small and Steve messed up—a lot. But slowly, things got better and the stages got bigger.

He went to Buffalo and tripped as the girls pulled him into their dance. In Milwaukee, he stayed on his feet and even managed to pose for photos with babies and their mothers. When he got to San Francisco, the stage was the biggest yet, and Steve felt proud when he walked through the flag and bent a pole into a red cross. With a smile, he handed it to a nurse in the audience and blushed when she batted her eyes at him.

The tour continued. Steve went to St. Louis

and Chicago, where film crews recorded his act. Later that night, he saw himself on the big screen, and for the first time he began to believe that maybe Senator Brandt was on to something. Steve had never actually fought in the war, but what the public didn't know couldn't hurt them.

In Philadelphia, a young boy came up to him with pen and paper in hand. "Hey, Cap," he said, his eyes wide as he took in his hero, "my brother says you took out four German tanks all by yourself."

Steve patted the boy on the head. "Sorry, kid. Tell your brother he's wrong." The boy's eyes filled with disappointment until Steve added, "It was *eight* German tanks." As the boy cheered, Steve grinned.

He was beginning to believe his own hype. There were Captain America comics and photos. He was on the big screen, and he played to sold-out theaters. He was a bona fide hero. There was nothing he couldn't do.

And then Steve was sent to the front line.

CHAPTER SEVEN

Captain America had taken his home country by storm, but Brandt wasn't satisfied. He wanted Steve to go to where the action was and energize the troops. Full of confidence and sure that he would be a star across the ocean, Steve flew over to Italy.

The US camp he was sent to was five miles from the front. When he got there, Steve took in the makeshift tents, the diverse troops, and the trucks that drove in and out at all hours carrying soldiers. It was nothing like the theaters and events back in America where they didn't know the true horrors of war.

After changing into his costume, Steve took his spot in the wings and waited for the dancing girls to do their part. Then, as he had done count-less times before, he stepped through the flag and shouted, "How many of you are ready to help me sock old Adolf in the jaw?"

He was met with silence.

Dozens of soldiers sat in their seats, glaring at him. Their uniforms were dirty and their faces lined with fatigue. Some of them had old wounds while others had fresh bandages on, having just returned from battle. Not one of them smiled at Steve.

Looking over his shoulder, he tried to find a way out. But there was no one waiting to signal him off the stage. So he forged on. "Okay," he said hesitantly, "I'm going to need a volunteer."

"I already volunteered," one of the soldiers shouted, his voice angry. "How do you think I got here?"

Steve opened his mouth to respond when another soldier shouted, "Bring back the girls."

The crowd began to boo and jeer. Steve was

taken aback. He had never experienced anything like this before.

As Steve retreated from the stage, the boos increased. Then tomatoes started flying. Holding up his shield, Steve blocked them. But it was a foolhardy effort. Even if none of the tomatoes hit him, he still felt like the biggest buffoon this side of the Atlantic.

A short while later, Steve sat in the empty bleachers, his head cradled in his hands. The soldiers had left, probably to go find real entertainment or talk about the real war and laugh at the man in the silly costume. Shame washed over Steve in huge waves. What had he been thinking? All this time he had fooled himself into believing he was a hero, a man of the people. But he was nothing but a joke. The men in the audience today were the real heroes. They had put their lives on the line time and time again, while all Steve had done was cheat his way to being a star. He hadn't even done anything with his superpowers since he had chased Kruger after the explosion. Had Erskine been wrong to think he was worthy? Had Phillips been right to doubt him?

The click of heels on the ground made Steve look up. He stifled a groan. Peggy Carter was walking toward him. He hadn't seen her since he had gone out on his "tour of duty," and he really didn't feel like seeing her now. She probably thought he was a joke, too. And he didn't want to see the disappointment in her beautiful eyes.

She took a seat next to him, and he met her gaze. He was surprised to see compassion there instead of disappointment, and his heart jumped in his chest. "I'm told you're quite the sensation back in the States," she said, her voice gentle.

Steve shrugged. "'America's new hope,'" he said bitterly, quoting one of the many newspaper headlines he'd read. Then he sighed. He shouldn't take out his frustration on Peggy. "You know," he went on, "all I dreamed about was coming overseas, being with the men on the lines, seeing you. And I finally get everything I wanted . . . and I'm wearing tights."

For a moment, Peggy didn't say anything. She wouldn't admit it out loud, but Steve's words had made her heart beat faster. He had wanted to see her? Did that mean what she thought it meant?

Shaking her head, she smiled at Steve. "I thought you looked dashing, but I rather did have a thing for Errol Flynn in *Robin Hood*," she said with a gleam in her eyes.

"The worst part is," Steve said, so lost in his own misery that he missed Peggy's obvious flirtation, "I was starting to buy it."

"None of us thought it would turn out like this," Peggy said. "But you've done well."

Steve knew that Peggy was only trying to help. Still, he was tired of thinking about Captain America, because every time he did a fresh wave of humiliation rolled over him. Changing the subject, he asked, "What about you?" He had been kept vaguely informed of what Peggy and Phillips had been doing since Kruger attacked the lab. He knew that they'd been chasing HYDRA. But he also knew that they had had little luck. From the look on Peggy's face, he knew the reports were right.

"We got word that Schmidt was moving a force through Azzano, testing some kind of new weaponry," she said after hesitating. "Two hundred men went in," she went on. "Less than fifty came back. Your adoring crowd tonight contained all that's left of the 107th."

Steve sat bolt upright. "107th?" he repeated.

Peggy nodded. "Yes, why?"

He didn't bother to explain. Pulling her up, Steve began hurrying her down the bleachers, heading toward the tents. He had to see Colonel Phillips—now. The 107th was Bucky's unit. And he hadn't been in the audience. Steve felt panic grip him. Had Bucky been captured? Or worse?

A few minutes later, Steve burst inside Phillips's tent. The colonel had arrived with Peggy after their last unsuccessful attempt to find HYDRA. Now he had the miserable task of going through the paperwork to see who had survived the Azzano attack. There were a lot of names to go through.

When Steve entered the tent, Phillips's eyes narrowed. He took in Steve's ridiculous costume and wondered, not for the first time, what Erskine had been thinking.

"I want to see the casualty list," Steve demanded.

Phillips raised an eyebrow. Then he pointed at the insignia on his collar stating his rank. Was this kid for real? Did he think that even with a fake title like "captain," he could order him around? But Steve wasn't going to be dissuaded.

"I don't need the whole list," he went on. "Just one name. Sergeant James Barnes. From the 107th."

There was a moment of strained silence as Steve glared at the colonel who glared right back. But then Peggy spoke up. "Sir, officially, Rogers is still SSR."

Phillips sighed. She was right. While the colonel didn't like it, Steve had the right to get this information. He began to leaf through the giant pile of papers in front of him. Each paper had the name, title, and contact information of a man who had been killed in the line of duty. "The name does sound familiar," he finally said. He couldn't find the paper now, but he was sure that Barnes was one of the casualties. "I'm sorry."

Steve paled. Bucky had died fighting while Steve had been playing a clown. It wasn't fair. Turning, Steve's eyes fell on one of the maps that Phillips had tacked to the wall. It showed aerial footage of a HYDRA facility. Given that the SSR had just lost men in the same vicinity, Steve figured this was where the prisoners of war were being held.

"What about the others?" he asked, turning back to the colonel. "You're planning a rescue mission, right?"

The colonel started in his seat, as though about to stand up and hit Steve for insubordination. But a glance from Peggy stopped him. Instead, he just said, "Yeah, it's called winning the war." The men from the 107th were a lost cause. Sending in a team to try and rescue them would only result in more casualties that the army couldn't afford.

"But if you know where they are—" Steve started to say, but Phillips stopped him.

"They're thirty miles behind the lines," he said. "Through some of the most heavily fortified territory in Europe. We'd lose more men than we'd save."

Then, with a nod, Phillips dismissed Steve.

Turning, Steve left the tent. Phillips may not have had any intention of rescuing those men, but Steve wasn't going to sit by and do nothing.

Not anymore. He'd figure out a way to get to that facility. He had to. He owed it to Bucky.

Steve grabbed one of the dancing girls' USA helmets—the one with the A on it—and dashed off. It was time for action. Captain America was about to go behind enemy lines to rescue captured American soldiers. Steve Rogers was finally going to war.

CHAPTER EIGHT

And so, later that night, Steve found himself inside the belly of a giant silver Lockheed Electra jet. On the bench across from him, Peggy Carter sat going over details of his seemingly impossible mission. In the cockpit, Howard Stark checked dials and instrument readings as he flew the plane further and further into enemy territory. He was the only pilot Peggy could find crazy enough to fly into enemy territory—and who didn't have to answer to Colonel Phillips.

Only Peggy and Stark knew what Steve was up to, and Steve shuddered at the thought of Phillips finding out. If discovered, he would surely be court-martialed and discharged from the army. But Steve wasn't about to just keep sitting around. He had seen the map. He had superstrength. And if he failed, Phillips would probably be happy to have Captain America out of his hair. Steve just wished Peggy hadn't put herself on the line for him.

"If I don't make it back, you're going to be in a lot of trouble," he said quietly, his voice just loud enough to carry above the whine of the engines.

Peggy didn't say it, but Steve was worth the risk. After all, she'd seen him try harder than anyone else back at Camp Lehigh, even when the odds were stacked against him. And now his best friend was presumed dead and others had been captured. Of course Peggy would help. She only wished he didn't have to do it all on his own.

Turning around in his seat, Stark smiled his charming smile. Unlike Steve and Peggy, he didn't seem bothered by the late-night stealth mission. In fact, he looked more confident and charming than usual.

"After we drop Steve off," he said, focusing

his handsome grin on Peggy, "I thought you and I could stop in Lucerne for late-night fondue."

Heat rushed to Peggy's cheeks as Steve raised an eyebrow. "Why is he saying fondue like that?" he asked. "What *is* fondue anyway? I don't like it."

Peggy grinned at the obvious jealousy in Steve's voice. "Stark's the best civilian pilot I've ever seen," she answered. "And mad enough to brave this airspace. We're lucky to have him."

"Have him?" Steve repeated, causing Peggy to grin even more. "Do you, are you two—?"

He was cut off by the sudden sound of gunfire. The plane lurched to the left as more guns hammered at its side. They were close to the drop zone, and HYDRA didn't want them there. Pulling on his parachute, Steve opened the jump door.

The plane tilted left and then right as Stark executed evasive maneuvers. Still, the side of the plane was getting pummeled with bullets. Steve had to get out of there now before they all went down.

"Once I'm clear, turn this thing around," he said, looking at Peggy, "and get out of here!"

"You can't give me orders," Peggy shouted over the howling wind.

Steve just smiled. "Yes I can. I'm a captain!"

And then, before she could say anything else, Steve jumped, disappearing from view.

The air rushed by, whipping Steve's hair and pulling at his clothes. Somewhere above him, he was vaguely aware that Stark had turned the plane around and was heading toward safer airspace. The guns went quiet, and Steve breathed a sigh of relief. Peggy and Stark would be okay.

Pulling his chute, Steve was momentarily jerked up as the wind caught the fabric and slowed him down. When he felt steady, Steve looked down, trying to see if he could spot a clear landing place. But the only thing he could see was the flash of gunfire as bullets flew through the air.

Pulling on the chords, Steve tried to steer the unwieldy chute away from the enemy fire, but it was no use. Bullets ripped through the chute, and Steve began falling faster and faster. Luckily, he had made it pretty close to the ground before the shooting started, and now the forest was only about twenty feet below. Unhooking himself, Steve used his shield to brace for impact as he plummeted to the ground. Crashing through the trees as they ripped at his clothes and scratched his face, Steve landed with a thud. The gunfire stopped as the enemy decided he'd never survive the fall. He was alive and behind enemy lines, mere miles from the HYDRA base.

It was time to go save some soldiers.

Moments later, Steve found himself outside the main gates to the HYDRA factory. It was just where Peggy said it would be. It was also just as heavily guarded as she had warned. Searchlights swept from several watchtowers along the perimeter, while thick barbed wire sat atop the wall surrounding the compound. Steve could make out the main factory building, which was billowing smoke while heavily armed HYDRA troopers marched back and forth across the grounds.

Steve needed a plan. Clearly he wasn't going to be able to just waltz right in there and ask for the prisoners back. The dark was suddenly illuminated by headlights as a convoy of three trucks pulled up to the gate. This was his break. As the driver of the first truck stopped to clear his entrance with the guard, Steve snuck over to the last vehicle and—making sure no one saw him—jumped inside and hid underneath a tarp. A moment later, the truck started up again and drove through the gate. Steve was in!

When he was sure that the coast was clear, Steve got out and slipped into the shadows. Now that he was inside the compound, he could make out more buildings and even more troopers.

All **STEVE ROGERS** ever wanted to do was fight for his country.

DR. ERSKINE sees that Steve has heart and determination, making him the best candidate for **PROJECT: REBIRTH**.

Meanwhile, across the globe, the evil **HYDRA** organization is on a quest for world domination.

HYDRA leader **JOHANN SCHMIDT** uncovers a mystical artifact of great power, which he believes comes from another world.

In a secret **SSR LAB**, Steve is placed into the **REBIRTH DEVICE**, where he will become America's first **SUPER-SOLDIER**.

AGENT PEGGY CARTER gives chase after a HYDRA spy destroys the SSR lab.

STEVE ROGERS transforms into the world's first
SUPER-SOLDIER, CAPTAIN AMERICA!

But Steve Rogers is not the only one who goes through a transformation.
JOHANN SCHMIDT IS NOW RED SKULL!

Steve is disappointed when **CAPTAIN AMERICA** turns into a stage show and not a soldier.

After Steve learns that **BUCKY** has been captured by HYDRA, Captain America springs into action to save his best friend.

HOWARD STARK offers Captain America a new shield made out of a rare metal called vibranium.

HYDRA AGENTS fight against Captain America and his Howling Commandos!

CAPTAIN AMERICA and **RED SKULL** clash in a fierce battle.

CAPTAIN AMERICA knows that his work as the world's first **SUPER-SOLDIER** will never end.

His eyes grew wide when he saw two HYDRA goons leading a long line of prisoners across the compound. Steve followed them to one of the barracks. As one of the guards brought the prisoners inside, the other stood at the door on watch. With one swift move, Steve took him out using a powerful roundhouse kick. Then he silently slipped into the prison.

As soon as his eyes adjusted to the dark, Steve's mouth dropped open in terror. The barracks were something out of a nightmare. Dozens of circular cages filled the space and each one overflowed with prisoners. There had to be hundreds of them. That meant HYDRA had captured more than just the 107th, Steve realized. He'd have to let Phillips know. But first, he needed to get them out.

There was a raised platform above the cages, and a guard was pacing back and forth on it. Quietly, Steve made his way up and then— CRACK! With a swift punch, he knocked out the guard, who then dropped off the platform and onto the cages below. The prisoners looked up, confused.

One of the men, a soldier by the name of Jones, watched as Steve stepped out of the shadows. He took in his helmet and shield. "Who are you supposed to be?" he asked.

"I'm Captain America." Steve answered, ignoring the groans that went up from the cages. He knew they had a right to doubt him. But he'd prove them wrong. Grabbing the key off the unconscious guard, he raced down the line of cages, opening each one. Dozens of men spilled out, shaking their numb limbs and stretching their sore muscles.

"Are there any others?" Steve asked when everyone was out.

"The isolation ward," a British soldier named Dum Dum Dugan answered. "On the factory floor."

Steve nodded. That was where he would go next.

Leaving the others to find weapons and a

way to distract the remaining guards, Steve made his way to the factory. The HYDRA troopers hadn't noticed that they were under attack—yet. But they would soon, and Steve still had men to rescue. Staying in the shadows, he ducked past trooper after trooper until he finally made it to the front door. Using his red-white-and-blue shield as an offensive weapon, he smashed two HYDRA guards in the face, knocking them out so he could make his way inside.

The factory floor was covered in weapons of war. There were hundreds of crates full of complete bombs and other crates with what looked like unfinished bombs. Inside even more crates, clusters of cartridges lay nestled in straw. Stepping closer, Steve noticed that the bombs and cartridges emitted a strange blue glow— just like the Super-Soldier serum. Pocketing one cartridge, he reminded himself to brief Phillips on this when—or rather, if—he got back to the base. Steve then cautiously continued through the bomb-making factory, heading toward the offices at the other end of the hangar.

But, unbeknownst to Steve, the factory wasn't just another HYDRA base, it was also Johann Schmidt's current headquarters. And he was watching everything Steve did over a closed-circuit camera. The HYDRA leader heard a loud explosion outside and turned to look at another monitor that revealed four prisoners blasting a hole in the factory wall. As the alarm blared and guards rushed out, Schmidt turned his attention back to the image of Steve. He watched as he punched and kicked his way past dozens of guards, getting closer and closer to Schmidt's office. It was an impressive—if annoying—sight.

"Doctor," Schmidt said, turning to his lead scientist, "prepare to evacuate."

The HYDRA scientist nervously eyed the camera, shifting between the action outside and the action inside the factory walls. "I'm sure our forces can handle—" he began.

"Our forces are outmatched," Schmidt snarled. "By one man," he added silently.

Looking down at the equipment panel in front of him, Schmidt flipped a switch and a countdown clock lit up. Then he slipped out the door and down the long corridor.

Steve had just made it into the corridor when he saw the scientist retreat and heard the door to the lab close. He didn't know who the man was, but by the way he kept glancing back at the door, Steve figured something important was in there. When the other man was out of sight, Steve slipped inside and shut the door behind him.

The lab was full of files and paperwork. Specimen jars lined shelves and various monitors beeped. In the middle of the room, a large cage sat atop a rusty drain. And inside the cage, Steve saw the back of a man, who was slumped on the ground.

Hearing footsteps, the man spoke up, his voice

scratchy. "Barnes, James Buchanan. Sergeant," he said.

Steve paused in midstep. It couldn't be . . .

"Bucky?" he said softly.

There was a moment of silence and then, "Who . . . who is that?"

Steve raced over and crouched down in front of the cage. Bucky was inside! He was beaten and grizzled, but he was alive. With one mighty swing, Steve smashed the lock. Then he held out his hand. "It's me, Buck."

"Steve?" Bucky said, taking in his old friend's new look.

"I thought you were dead," Steve said.

"I thought you were smaller," Bucky replied as Steve hauled him to his feet and helped him out of the cage. When they were both standing, Bucky stared up at his friend, his eyes disbelieving. This wasn't the Steve he knew. This Steve was bigger, faster, and stronger than the scrawny kid Bucky grew up with in Brooklyn. And now, in a startling turn of events, Steve was about to save Bucky.

"What happened to you?" Bucky finally asked.

"I joined the army," Steve answered matter-of-factly.

Suddenly, a blast rocked the room. One of the machines on the factory floor was triggered to explode, and it sent Steve and Bucky hurtling. They would have to catch up later. Right now, they had to get out of there.

Putting an arm around Bucky, Steve began to lead him from the room. Out of the corner of his eye, Steve spotted a map on one of the walls. He paused, noticing that it was covered in HYDRA symbols that spread all across Europe. He took a mental picture of the map and then, as another explosion rocked the building, moved back into the hall with Bucky.

All around them, bombs continued to go off, shaking the foundation of the factory and making it hard to move quickly. As they made their way down the corridor, Bucky continued trying to get answers. He figured Steve must have undergone some kind of treatment or been in an experiment. There was no way he could have naturally changed into the man who stood next to him. "Did it hurt?" he asked.

"Little bit," Steve answered, dodging a piece of ceiling as it crashed to the ground.

"Is it permanent?"

"So far," Steve said.

They had reached a stairwell that led either up to a catwalk or down, back toward the factory floor. Steve started to lead them down when another series of explosions ripped through the building. A huge chunk of wall fell onto the stairs, blocking their way. It looked as if they were going to have to head up.

Dragging the still-weak Bucky, Steve got them up onto the catwalk. Outside, he heard shouts as the escaping prisoners fought against the HYDRA soldiers. More bombs went off, making Steve's ears ring. When the smoke cleared, he noticed that someone was blocking their way.

"Captain America. How exciting," Johann Schmidt said, a sneer on his face. In his hand he held what looked like a titanium box. "I'm a fan of your films," he went on. He handed the box to the man in the lab coat Steve had seen earlier. Then Schmidt moved forward. Steve took a step forward as well.

"So, the old man managed it after all," Schmidt continued. "Not quite an improvement, but impressive."

Anger filled Steve as Schmidt spoke. With a cry of rage, he pulled back his arm and punched Schmidt as hard as he could. The HYDRA leader went stumbling backward. "You've got no idea what you're talking about," Steve said.

A smile played over Schmidt's face and he looked almost pleased by Steve's reaction. "Don't I?" he asked. Then he swung. Thinking quickly, Steve threw up his mighty shield, blocking the punch. When he lowered the shield, there was a fist-size dent in it. Steve looked up, confused. A moment later, Schmidt hit him, knocking him to the ground.

"Erskine said your experiment was a failure," Steve said, trying to catch his breath. He kicked his legs, driving his feet hard into Schmidt's jaw.

Seeing his leader on the ground, the HYDRA scientist raced over to the catwalk controls. Flipping a switch, the sides began to retract, creating a gap between the fighting men.

Meanwhile, Steve and Schmidt had gotten back to their feet. When Steve looked over at the HYDRA leader, his jaw dropped. It looked as if Schmidt's face was on crooked. Red muscle seemed to bulge out of torn seams in Schmidt's head, as if his sinister self could no longer be contained by human skin.

"A failure?" Schmidt said. "Oh, no, Captain. I was his greatest success." Then, with an evil grin, Schmidt reached up—and pulled off his face! Underneath, there was nothing but a gruesome red skull!

As Steve and Bucky gaped at the horrific sight, Schmidt let out a diabolical laugh. Then, turning, he slipped into a nearby elevator. A moment later, the doors slammed shut. Schmidt had escaped, but Steve and Bucky were trapped.

Another series of explosions rocked the building, and the catwalk shuddered beneath Steve and Bucky. There was no time to worry about the HYDRA leader now. They had to get out of there, or they were going to end up falling to their deaths. Before Bucky could protest, Steve picked him up and threw him across the gap between the two sides of the catwalk. He was about to follow him when—BOOM! BOOM! BOOM! More explosions caused the catwalk to split even wider. Steve was left stranded on one side while Bucky waited for him on the other.

"Just get out!" Steve shouted to his friend.

"Not without you!" Bucky shouted back as the roof began to collapse.

Steve looked around. The only way out was

on the other side of the catwalk. He raced back as far as he could to give himself a running start and then took off. He was going to jump! He ran faster and faster. When he reached the edge, he gave himself one last push and leaped—just as the biggest bomb went off.

Bucky watched in horror as Steve disappeared into the flames.

CHAPTER NINE

Colonel Phillips sat in front of his typewriter, his fingers hesitating over the keys. Taking a deep breath, he continued his note: "Senator Brandt. Regret to report Cpt. Steven Rogers K.I.A." He stopped typing as Peggy Carter came to the door.

She looked tired and sad. In her hand, she held aerial photographs of the destroyed HYDRA camp. "No sign of activity," she reported.

Phillips stared at her, his expression cold. She had disobeyed direct orders and helped Steve on his ill-fated mission. While Phillips had never really liked Steve, he didn't think the kid should have been put in a situation like that. He wasn't equipped to handle it—even if he had a "captain" before his name.

"I can't touch Stark," Phillips said after a tense moment of silence. "He's a civilian. And a rich one. *You* are neither."

Peggy nodded. She had expected that reaction. And frankly, she didn't care. Not anymore. Not with Steve dead. "You'll have my resignation in the morning," she said. She paused, as if not sure whether to go on. "With respect, sir, I don't regret my actions. And I doubt Captain Rogers did either."

"I took a chance on you," Phillips said, untouched by her words. "Now America's golden boy—and a lot of other men—are dead. Because you had a *crush*."

The response on the tip of Peggy's tongue died at the sound of a commotion outside. Soldiers were running by, shouting to each other excitedly. Walking to the window, Peggy and Phillips looked out. The gates to the camp were opening. And beyond them—battered and bruised but very much alive—was Captain America.

Steve and Bucky walked slowly up the road, leading the squad of rescued soldiers back to their Italian home. A ragtag group of vehicles followed farther behind, carrying the wounded and weak.

Once inside the base, Steve pushed through the growing crowd and made his way over to Phillips and Peggy. "Colonel," he said, his tone weary, "some of these men need medical attention." Phillips nodded and Steve went on. "I'd like to surrender myself for disciplinary action."

The colonel looked at Steve, then at the soldiers stumbling into the camp, and then back at Steve. Despite the bruises and scratches all over his body, Steve's eyes were alert. The events at the factory had changed him. He wasn't the same man who had gone beyond enemy lines. He had faced real danger—and survived.

"That won't be necessary," Phillips finally said.

"Sir, I—"

"Just how many orders do you plan on disobeying," Phillips barked, "Captain?"

Then he walked away, leaving Steve open-mouthed with shock. Phillips had called him "Captain." He had finally proven himself to the toughest man he knew. Turning, his eyes met Peggy's. There was a jolt of electricity, and Steve felt his heart begin to race. There was so much he wanted to say to her. But she beat him to it. "You said you'd call," she stated.

He smiled. That was probably the closest he was going to get to a welcome home from Peggy. But he'd take it. "Didn't think you'd have room for us all," he said, teasing her.

Before he could say more, soldiers crowded around him, clapping him on the back and congratulating him. Peggy moved to the side as they began to chant his name. Steve couldn't keep the smile from his face. For the first time since he'd donned the Captain America costume, he truly felt like a hero. And it felt good.

A few days later, Steve attended a briefing at the London headquarters of the SSR. A newspaper headline lying on one of the tables read: CAPTAIN AMERICA TO RECEIVE MEDAL OF HONOR.

However, Steve had no interest in attending the ceremony. He was too busy. As Peggy and Stark looked on, Steve sketched out the precise coordinates of the HYDRA bases he had seen back in Schmidt's office.

"Forty degrees, twenty-three minutes north," he said. Then, looking over at the other two, he added, "I only got a quick look."

Peggy smiled. Since he had returned from the HYDRA camp, things had changed between them. They both felt a spark lying just below the surface, ready to ignite. "Nobody's perfect," she said, her eyes twinkling.

Just then, Colonel Phillips entered. Walking over, he glanced at the map on the table and then at the blue cartridge Steve had taken from the

HYDRA factory. "You figure out what this is yet?" Phillips asked.

Howard Stark had suffered through Steve and Peggy's flirting for far too long. Eager for a diversion, he answered, "The most powerful explosive known to man, according to Rogers." There was a hint of bitterness in Stark's voice. He prided himself on inventing the most powerful things. He didn't like it that he'd been beaten to the punch. Taking out a pair of tweezers, he gingerly picked up the cartridge.

"Either Schmidt's darn near rewritten the laws of physics," he went on, "or this isn't from—" He couldn't say it out loud. It seemed impossible that Schmidt's delusional belief in gods and other worlds could have any basis in fact. He shook his head. "I can *say* that if they've got enough of it, this war isn't going the way anyone thinks it is."

The room fell silent as Stark's words sank in. They were at a critical point in the war. If this cartridge was just one of many, then the results would be worldwide annihilation—and HYDRA domination.

Walking over to the map, Phillips began tracing the various *x*'s that marked the HYDRA camps. "Then we'd better take it away from them," he finally said. "These are all HYDRA's factories?"

Steve put down his pencil and shook his head. "Not all of them," he answered. "Bucky—I mean Sergeant Barnes—said HYDRA shipped all the bombs somewhere else. Somewhere *not* on this map."

Bucky overheard a lot while he'd been kept in the cage in HYDRA's science lab. He filled Steve in on as much as he could remember during the trek back from the factory. This piece of information was the most important of all.

The room fell silent again as they all processed the news that there were more bombs out there. Bombs of otherworldly power. They needed to get their hands on them before Schmidt had the chance to use them. And while they didn't know where the majority of the bombs were being shipped, thanks to Steve's map they *did* know where the other HYDRA bases were. Maybe destroying them would put Schmidt on edge and give SSR the advantage.

Turning to face Steve, Colonel Phillips smiled. "What do you say, Rogers? It's your map. Think you can wipe HYDRA off of it?"

Steve returned the smile. There was nothing he would like to do more. And he had the perfect team in mind to help him. . . .

———————⊙———————

The Whip and Fiddle was a local London pub that served cold drinks, warm food, and good cheer. That night, it was full of the soldiers Steve had helped rescue from the HYDRA factory. Making his way through the crowd, Steve found Bucky in the back, leaning against a barstool. Four other men—Falsworth, Jones, Dernier, Morita, and Dugan—stood a bit to the side. Since rescuing them, these men had become Steve's friends and, he hoped, they'd now become his teammates.

"Let me get this straight," Dugan said after Steve explained the mission. "You want us to march back into combat against the same guys who handed us our butts last time?"

"Yes," Steve answered, nodding.

Dum Dum Dugan shrugged. "Sounds good," he said. The other three nodded in agreement, and Steve tried not to laugh. That had been easier than he expected. Now he had the rest of the night to have a good time before they set out in the morning.

Turning, he joined Bucky at the bar. "What about you," Steve asked when they were alone. "You ready to follow Captain America into the jaws of death?"

To Steve's surprise, Bucky shook his head.

"No," he answered, and Steve's mouth dropped open. Then Bucky added, "The little shrimp— the kid in the alley who couldn't stay down, and wouldn't take no for an answer? *That's* the guy I'm following."

Steve smiled at his old friend.

They were still talking about strategy and the mission when Steve looked up and saw Peggy making her way through the crowd. She had traded her usual uniform for a striking red dress and looked beautiful. Noticing that his friend was distracted, Bucky turned and saw Peggy. He smiled. Not bad.

Joining them, Peggy informed Steve that he had an early morning meeting with Stark. Apparently, the inventor had been working day and night to create some new equipment and needed Steve to come by and try it out. Then she noticed Falsworth and Jones were standing in the middle of the room, singing at the top of their lungs. Dernier and Morita looked on, laughing as the two men tried to pull a couple of girls in for a dance.

"I see your crack squad is prepping for duty," she observed.

Bucky gave Peggy one of his trademark grins. The one that had caused plenty of Brooklyn girls to go weak at the knees. "You don't like music?" he asked playfully.

"I do actually," Peggy answered, looking not at Bucky but at Steve. "I may even, when this is all over, go dancing."

The music grew louder, but it seemed that Peggy and Steve couldn't hear it. They just continued to look at one another, as though having a silent conversation. Growing tired of it, Bucky held out a hand and said, "Then what are you waiting for?"

Dragging her gaze from Steve, Peggy turned to Bucky and put a gentle hand on his arm. "The right partner," she answered, clearly meaning Steve. Then, with one last look at Steve, she turned and left.

When she was gone, Bucky groaned. "I'm invisible!" he cried. Then a realization struck him and he laughed. "Oh, God, I've turned into you."

Steve gave him a wicked smile. "Don't take it so hard," he said teasingly. "Maybe she's got a friend."

As Bucky stormed off, Steve just stood there with a smile on his face. True, he was about to go on a dangerous mission. But things suddenly felt really good. He had his best friend back, a great team to rely on, and maybe, just maybe, a future with Peggy. For the first time in a long while, things were beginning to look up.

CHAPTER TEN

The next morning, Steve reported to Stark's office as requested. But when he got there, Stark had not yet arrived. A beautiful young blond woman sitting behind a desk informed Steve that the inventor would be there in a minute. Then she introduced herself as Private Lorraine.

"The women of America owe you their thanks," she said, getting up and walking over to Steve. "And seeing as they're not here . . ." Before Steve knew what was happening, Private Lorraine leaned in and kissed him. For a moment he protested, but then he gave in and kissed her back.

Steve didn't want to be kissing this woman, he wanted to be kissing Peggy—who was now standing right there! She had entered the office midkiss, and the look on her face now could have turned a man to stone. Turning, she stormed out the door. Steve followed, hot on her heels.

"Agent Carter!" he called. "Wait a second!"

But it was no use. She wanted nothing to do with him.

Sighing, Steve turned and went back into Stark's office to wait. So maybe things weren't going as well as he thought.

A few minutes later, Howard Stark finally showed up. After giving Private Lorraine a grin, he led Steve down to his lab where technicians were busy unwrapping various pieces of equipment. Others were installing futuristic machines like those Steve had seen back at the World Exhibition of Tomorrow. Peggy stood to one side, her arms crossed.

Ignoring everyone else, Stark walked over to

a slightly-less-cluttered section of the lab. Lying on a table was what looked like a bodysuit. Steve cocked his head. What on earth was it?

"Steel micromesh for the sleeves," Stark explained, pointing to the suit's arms. "Titanium panels for your more vulnerable parts. Chest plates . . . and such."

Steve's eyes grew wide as Stark moved down the table and picked up a gray-colored material. He was getting his very own, state-of-the-art combat suit. "Carbon polymer," Stark went on. "It's flexible, insulated, fire-resistant, and ought to hold its own against your average military-grade trench knife. But not against a bullet or anything HYDRA's got."

And that's when Stark presented Steve with the biggest surprise of all. Eyeing the beat-up shield Steve held in his hand, Stark walked over to a cart full of half-built shields. Some of them had gadgets on them, one had lights, and another looked like it had been painted with camouflage.

"I tinkered with a few ideas for improvements. But in the end . . ." He pulled away a tarp covering one portion of the cart. ". . . I thought we'd keep it simple."

Lying on the cart was a mighty shield. It didn't have any gadgets or lights or hidden compartments. Instead, it was lightweight, balanced, and almost indestructible. It was the perfect offensive and defensive symbol of the United States of America, and it would become Captain America's most trusted and well-known weapon. Cautiously, Steve reached out and ran a hand across the shield's smooth surface. Then he gave it a tap, and it rang like a bell.

"Vibranium," Stark informed them. "A hundred times stronger than steel and one third the weight." Picking it up, Steve slid the shield onto his arm as Stark continued. "It's completely vibration absorbent. Should make a bullet feel like a cotton ball."

Steve smiled. This was the coolest thing

ever. Turning, he asked Peggy what she thought.

In answer, she pulled out her gun and fired—right at him. The slug hit the shield and flattened out, plunking harmlessly to the ground. "I think it works," she said. Then she stalked out of the room.

Steve gulped. He had some serious explaining to do.

But it would have to wait. Right now, he had to go after HYDRA.

He just hoped that Peggy would forgive him by the time he came back.

CHAPTER ELEVEN

For the next few months, Captain America and his ragtag unit of Howling Commandos traveled all over Europe, chasing down and destroying as many HYDRA bases as they could find.

First, they headed to France. This was one of the weaker HYDRA stations, and in no time, the team took it over. Back at their headquarters, Peggy replaced one of the x's with an SSR flag.

Then they headed to Poland, where Bucky took out the guard at the front gate so the team could enter. As the others streamed past them, he and Steve traded knowing smiles. It was just like being back in Brooklyn—only slightly more dangerous. Another SSR flag was pinned on the map.

Next up was a base in Czechoslovakia.

Signaling for the others to wait, Captain America made his way inside by himself. Ducking and weaving past the HYDRA troopers, he found the collection of bombs. He quickly placed a detonator among them and then grabbed one of the trooper's bikes, jumped on it, and raced away. He barely managed to crash through a factory window before the place exploded behind him. Another base destroyed.

The rest of the team was having fun taking revenge against the organization that had held them prisoner. In Greece, Dernier set another explosive charge and—BOOM!—the place blew to bits. Pinned down in Germany, Morita shouted coordinates to Jones over a handheld radio. Jones quickly fired his weapon while at the same time Falsworth threw a grenade. The base exploded. Another HYDRA camp down.

The team's wave of destruction did not go

unnoticed. Johann Schmidt had taken refuge in a secret Greek camp, one of the few remaining HYDRA strongholds. Standing in front of his troop leaders, Schmidt, now known to his followers as Red Skull, raged on. "We are close to an offensive that will shake the planet," he said angrily. "Yet we are continually delayed because you can't outwit a clown dressed in a flag!"

This was unacceptable. Captain America and his Howling Commandos needed to be taken out. Fast. For the first time since the attacks began, Red Skull's evil smile returned. He had come up with a good idea. An idea that would take care of Captain America—once and for all.

Unaware of Red Skull's plans, Cap, Bucky, and the rest of the team gathered on a plateau high above a Russian valley. The sun was not up yet, and the wind was cold as it whipped around them.

Steve was nervous. There had been no base in this area marked on the map. Which meant it was either a trap or a huge find. Using one of the HYDRA code transceivers they'd stolen from a captured base, they had intercepted a transmission claiming that a large HYDRA train was on the move through a nearby Alpine pass and that HYDRA's top scientist was on board. Steve had made the decision to act. It was risky to go into unknown territory, but this might be the chance they needed to finish off HYDRA once and for all.

As Jones listened to another transmission, Dugan and Falsworth kept a lookout on the valley below. Meanwhile, Cap, Bucky, and Dernier moved closer to the edge.

"The train engineer just radioed ahead," Jones called out. "HYDRA gave him permission to open the throttle. Wherever their base is, he's trying to make it there by dawn." He paused and then added, "With their biggest shipment yet."

Just then, a train whistle blew, piercing the silence of the night. Looking through his binoculars, Dugan saw a large, futuristic-looking train racing down the tracks. Turning, he nodded at Steve. It was time.

Quickly, Dernier helped Cap, Bucky, and Jones strap into harnesses. Then he snapped three hooks onto a long cable that stretched out over the pass. This was how they were going to get on the train. But they had to time it just right. If they didn't, they'd either be crushed by the train—or by the opposite wall of the valley.

The train whistle blew again and Captain America nodded at his men. Now! Together, they pushed off, zipping down toward the oncoming train. For a moment, it looked as if they were going to miss, but then with a THUD! they landed on the slick roof. Unhooking themselves, they let the cable fly away. They didn't want to leave any evidence of their presence.

As planned, Jones headed toward the engine

of the train. His mission was to somehow stop the train so the rest of the team would have enough time to get down there. Steve and Bucky, meanwhile, were going after the explosives.

Jumping down into the train, the friends found themselves in the first car. It was empty. Moving into the next car, they exchanged looks. It was empty, too. This didn't seem right. Cautiously, they entered the next car. Unlike the others, this car was pitch dark. And eerily quiet. Steve couldn't even hear the sound of the rushing wind outside. Then, WHAM! Behind them, a steel plate dropped down, blocking the back door.

A moment later, the lights flickered on. It was a trap! Standing in front of them was the largest HYDRA trooper Steve had ever seen. The monster of a man was easily over six and a half feet tall, and instead of arms, he had two huge, robotic cannons attached to his shoulders. It was the perfect plan. Red Skull had lured Captain

America here so that this *thing* could kill him.

Steve shook his head in revolt. He and his men had come too far to let that happen. Pulling out his gun, Cap opened fire, but the bullets just zinged harmlessly off the trooper's armor. Then, as Steve watched in horror, the trooper raised one of its cannon "arms," aimed, and fired. *BLAM!* A blue energy pulse sent Steve flying into the side-wall of the train, knocking the breath out of him.

Then the trooper turned and aimed at Bucky. Another burst came from the cannon and Bucky barely managed to duck out of the way. The blue energy missed him and blasted a huge hole in the side of the train. Outside, the valley walls rushed by as the train continued to speed on. Struggling to his feet, Captain America held up his shield and started to advance on the giant trooper. Once again, the HYDRA agent held up one of his cannon arms. The weapon hummed as the blue energy filled it and the trooper leveled it out— aiming right for the star on Steve's chest.

The blue energy burst out of the cannon in a steady stream. But Cap lifted his shield just in the nick of time, and the energy hit it instead of him. With determined steps, Captain America pushed against the stream of energy, getting closer and closer to the trooper. Then, with one last mighty shove, he pushed the shield out in front of him, sending all the blue energy right back at the HYDRA agent, causing him to flow back through the gaping hole in the train car and disappear from view.

Steve collapsed to the ground. Suddenly, there was a shout from the other side of the train car. Steve sprinted over just as a side door opened. There, with a grin plastered across his face, was Jones. He was holding HYDRA's lead scientist in front of him. HYDRA's plan to trap and destroy Captain America and his Howling Commandos had failed. The heroes had succeeded!

CHAPTER TWELVE

Captain America and his team made their way back to London headquarters. Phillips had ordered them to bring the scientist right to him. It was time to get answers.

It didn't take long to break the weasly man. He sat bound to a chair, sweat dripping down his face. "Schmidt believes he walks in the footsteps of gods," the scientist told Phillips. "Only the entire world will satisfy him."

Phillips scoffed. The HYDRA leader had a few screws loose, but he posed a serious threat nevertheless. "What's his target?" the colonel asked.

"Everywhere," the HYDRA agent answered vaguely.

After a few more hours of interrogation, Phillips had all the information he was going to get. He met with Peggy and ran through what he had learned. Then he called the others into the conference room. When everyone was settled, he began. "Johann Schmidt belongs in the bughouse," he said. "He thinks he's a god, and he's going to blow up half the world to prove it."

Peggy stood up and walked over to a map of the world. "Starting with the United States." The room grew silent as everyone processed the news. Peggy went on. "Schmidt's working with powers beyond our capabilities. He gets across the Atlantic, he'll wipe out the entire eastern seaboard in an hour." As she spoke, she looked directly at Steve. Since he had returned from his latest mission, he had been withdrawn and quiet. They did not have the opportunity to talk about what had happened with Private Lorraine, and now it seemed they might never have the chance.

A shiver of fear ran through her as she thought about what this latest intel meant for Steve—and for her.

As Peggy spoke, everyone in the room turned and looked at the map, their eyes focusing on New York City. They were each thinking the same thing. The United States was completely defenseless against an attack of that magnitude. The majority of soldiers had been deployed to Europe or the Pacific. Schmidt was heading across the Atlantic—they had to act fast.

"How much time have we got?" Dernier asked.

Phillips looked grave. "Under twenty-four hours."

No one said anything for a moment. They had just returned from fighting HYDRA and were tired, having been pushed to their limits. But they couldn't sit around and do nothing.

"Where is Red Skull now?" Steve asked, standing up.

"HYDRA's last base is here, in the Alps," Phillips said, pointing to the map. Then he traced his finger down as he added, "Five hundred feet below the surface."

Steve nodded. This wasn't going to be easy. But they could do it. They *had* to do it. Looking at the rest of his team, he saw that they had the same determination in their eyes that he probably did.

Captain America and the Howling Commandos were heading to the Alps.

CHAPTER THIRTEEN

Cap and his team worked quickly to prepare for their next—and hopefully last—mission. Stark outfitted them with equipment capable of taking out HYDRA's defenses and of protecting them from enemy fire. While Steve gave the rest of the team a few hours off to relax and recharge, Peggy and Phillips briefed him on the layout of the base and the surrounding landscape. He would be taking the lead in the attack. The others would follow him once he was in, providing backup and, if necessary, an escape route. The part of the base that was aboveground would be well guarded, but it would still be easy for Captain America to sneak in. The tricky part would be finding Red Skull amid the labyrinthine corridors and rooms deep below the surface. The SSR didn't have specific information on where the HYDRA leader would be holing up inside. Steve would be going in blind.

But he wasn't worried. In fact, he had a plan that he hadn't shared with Peggy or Phillips. If everything went as he suspected it would, Red Skull would come to him. . . .

Soon, everything was in place. The team, including Peggy and Phillips, took a plane to a designated spot a few dozen miles from the base. Their hope was to land undetected, which would give Steve a head start. After that, it was up to him.

A few hours after landing, Captain America raced his motorcycle through the dense forest near the HYDRA base. His team was behind him, getting ready for their part, and Steve was running on pure adrenaline. He was finally going to take Red

Skull down and make the evil man pay for all the death and destruction he had been responsible for. Whatever happened today, Captain America had only one goal—to face Red Skull alone.

He was so focused on Schmidt that he didn't notice when his bike unwittingly tripped a wire lying across the small road. Nearby, in a secret HYDRA outpost, a warning light blinked. Seeing it, two HYDRA guards leaped onto their bikes and headed toward the road. Soon, they had caught up to Steve.

The sound of roaring engines caused Cap to turn just as the HYDRA troopers drove onto the road. They were just a few feet behind him, and gaining fast. Revving his engine, Captain America shot forward. But the sentries were too close; they gained on him. Before he could maneuver away, one of them jerked his handlebars to the left, sideswiping Cap's bike. The motorcycle wobbled, but Steve managed to steady it. Then he quickly jerked his wheel to the right, causing him to careen into the trooper. There was the sound of metal crunching as the bike frames crashed into each other.

Captain America needed to get rid of this trooper. Looking up ahead, he smiled. It seemed he'd just found a way. Gunning his engine, he hunched low over the handlebars and sped forward, the trooper staying right behind him. Then, at the last moment, Cap dropped his bike into a slide—ducking below a low-hanging branch. The trooper didn't have time to react and—WHACK!—he hit the branch head-on. The HYDRA agent went flying, his bike exploding in the fiery crash.

There was no time to celebrate taking down the guard. Gunshots rang out as the other trooper pulled his pistol and began firing. Cap ducked and wove his bike down the road, trying to stay out of the way of the flying bullets. But he couldn't keep it up forever. Thinking quickly, he slammed on his brakes, the tires screeching on the pavement. In moments, the trooper caught up with him. When he did, Cap grabbed the handlebars on the other bike. Using all his super-strength, he clung tightly as the trooper swerved back and forth across the road. Steve stuck like glue. Seeing a huge pine tree ahead, Steve jerked the sentry's bike toward it. Just before they were about to crash, Steve turned at the last possible second, saving himself from certain death. But the HYDRA agent couldn't get away. His bike slammed into the pine and exploded.

Steve smiled. Two down, a few more to go. It was time to get inside the HYDRA base.

The HYDRA base stood high on a mountaintop in the Alps, its buildings protected by a large wall covered in barbed wire. Alarms were already sounding as Captain America approached, but he didn't care. This was all part of his plan. The plan he hadn't told Peggy or Phillips about. But he did tell the Howling Commandos about it, and hopefully they were at the ready.

When he was about twenty feet away from the wall, Cap gunned his bike's engine. A few feet later, he pulled back on the handlebars. As the engine groaned under the effort, he jumped the bike up and over the wall. He landed with a thud safely on the other side.

HYDRA troopers immediately opened fire as Steve tore across the compound. With lightning-quick reflexes, he stayed ahead of the bullets—until one hit his tire. With a loud pop, the tire blew out, sending Steve flying over the handlebars. He hit the ground hard but got to his feet, fists swinging as the HYDRA troopers closed in. But there were just too many of them. They over-powered him.

Captain America had been captured.

A few minutes later, Captain America found himself tied up inside Johann Schmidt's office. Red Skull circled him, with a sneer on his face. Schmidt would make the hero watch as he destroyed his beloved country.

Schmidt's office was dark and oppressive. On one wall, a large picture of Schmidt, with his red skull showing in all its hideous glory, was displayed. Steve didn't know whether it was supposed to serve as a warning to those who entered, or whether Schmidt was so crazy he just liked to look at his disfigured face.

Noticing Captain America's gaze, Red Skull leaned in closer. "That is why you are here?" he asked. "To finish this face-to-face?"

"Against your face?" Cap retorted. "I wouldn't stand a chance."

Red Skull growled and savagely booted Captain America in the head, knocking him off balance. Then he spun him around and slammed him face-first into the hard concrete floor. "A sensible man would lie down," Red Skull said. "The more you fight, the more painful your death will be," he threatened.

Captain America ignored Red Skull's words. Struggling, he turned and tried to kick Schmidt, but Steve was in an awkward position and the kick went wide. Grabbing Cap's foot, the HYDRA leader swung Captain America into a wall, instantly knocking the wind out of him. But Captain America wasn't ready to give up yet.

"I can do this all day," Steve said, breathing heavily.

"I believe you can," Red Skull replied. He pulled out his pistol and aimed it at Steve's head, his hand steady. "But I am on a schedule."

Captain America didn't look scared or upset. In fact, he looked . . . happy?

"So am I," he said, just as the office window behind him shattered. Falsworth and the rest of the Howling Commandos crashed into the room, swinging from ropes and firing their weapons.

Using the distraction to his advantage, Captain America rose to his feet and barreled into Red Skull. The HYDRA leader went flying into the far wall, leaving a human-size dent in it. Meanwhile, explosions rocked the base above.

"You lose your whole base just to give me a beating?" Steve said. "Sloppy."

Rage filled Schmidt's red face, turning it even redder. Reaching out, he gave Captain America a one-two punch that sent him flying backward. As he tried to recover, Schmidt raced across the room and grabbed a titanium box. It was the same one that Steve had seen back when he had rescued Bucky. Whatever was inside must be important to Schmidt, he thought. Steve planned on taking it from the HYDRA leader before destroying him.

As Steve watched, Schmidt bolted from the room. The rest of Steve's team had taken care of the HYDRA troopers who had tried to fight them and were now cleaning up the mess. Picking up Cap's shield, Falsworth handed it to him and watched as Steve used the sharp edge to break his shackles. At the same moment, more guards entered and fired their weapons. The Howling Commandos surrounded a HYDRA agent who fumbled for his cyanide capsule. "Cut off one head, two more shall rise—" the agent began to say.

Just then, a BLAM! finished the trooper's sentence as he fell to the ground. Colonel Phillips strode through the base, machine gun in hand, and addressed the Howling Commandos. "Then let's go find two more . . ." he said. Confident that the colonel and the Howling Commandos could handle the rest of the HYDRA troopers, Steve turned and raced down the corridor.

Captain America was going after Red Skull.

CHAPTER FOURTEEN

The underground base was full of corridors that twisted and turned, making it easy to get lost. Turning a corner, Captain America saw Red Skull up ahead, the box still clutched tightly in his hand. He put on a burst of speed. Hearing footsteps, Red Skull turned and pulled out a gun. It looked a lot like the one Steve had seen on the train. As he watched, it filled with blue energy and the blast came straight at him. Quickly, Cap raised his vibranium shield, and the blue energy bounced off it in a brilliant flash of light.

With a roar of frustration, Schmidt began running again. Steve followed him until they came to a four-way intersection. The HYDRA leader dashed through the doorway straight ahead. Then, turning, he gave Steve another evil sneer. Reaching over, he pressed a button, and a large blast door began to lower.

There was no way Captain America was going to let Red Skull get away. Not when he was this close to taking down the HYDRA leader. Pulling his arm back, he flung his mighty shield straight at the closing door. THUNK! It jammed the door, leaving enough room for Steve to crawl under.

Standing up on the other side, he looked around. There was nowhere to go but straight ahead. He quickly began running down the corridor only to come to a screeching halt. Standing in front of him, holding two weapons that looked like huge flamethrowers, stood a HYDRA trooper. The trooper had a tank, filled to the top with the powerful and deadly blue substance, strapped to his back. Steve gulped. This wasn't good.

Raising the twin guns, the trooper pulled a trigger. On his back, the tank gurgled and whined as it sent fiery blue energy through the tubes and into the guns. Cap lifted his hand, prepared to use his shield to protect himself once more. But then he remembered. He'd left it back at the intersection! He was completely defenseless. The trooper fired blue energy at Steve. The Super-Soldier braced himself for the impact, hoping his superstrength might make him fireproof when—BOOM!—the wall behind the trooper exploded and a blast knocked the energy canister off his back.

A huge tank rolled into the hall. Behind the wheel was Peggy Carter. "You're late," Steve said, smiling at her. He had never been so happy to see anyone in his life. Peggy smiled back at him, her eyes warm. With a wave of thanks, Captain America took off after Red Skull.

At the end of the hall, Steve came to another doorway. Racing through it, he found himself inside a giant hangar built deep into the mountain. A rumbling filled the air. As Steve watched, a gigantic plane rolled past. But this was no normal plane. It was at least four times the size of the biggest U.S. Army plane and looked to be outfitted with numerous guns. Looking around, Steve noticed that there were five more just like it! These must be the planes that Schmidt was going to use to attack the United States. They're big enough to carry the blue bombs and thousands of HYDRA troopers, he realized.

Looking back at the plane that was making its way down the hangar, Steve saw Schmidt sitting in the cockpit. The HYDRA leader turned and smiled. Steve couldn't stop him now. The plane began moving faster and faster.

"Where are you going to go?" Steve asked out loud. "There's no way out." But he'd spoken to soon. At the other end of the hangar, giant doors began to open, letting in the glare of sunlight. This wasn't just a hangar, it was a runway!

Captain America started running, but it was no use. Red Skull was too far ahead. Steve was fast, but not as fast as a giant plane. His fists pumped at his sides as he tried harder and harder to pick up speed. He was just about to give up when the sound of a car engine came from right next to him. Looking over, Steve saw Colonel Phillips sitting behind the wheel of Schmidt's classic German car. Peggy was in the backseat, holding Cap's shield.

Quickly, Steve leaped inside the car as Phillips stepped on the gas, sending them shooting forward. In moments, they had caught up with the plane. The car shuddered as Phillips pulled it up next to the plane's large back tire. The wheel was attached to a long metal landing gear that extended up to the inside of the plane itself.

Captain America was about to pull himself through the window and onto the wheel of the plane when Peggy let out a shout. "Wait!" she cried. Then, before Steve knew what was happening, she pulled him into a kiss. For a moment,

Steve forgot about Schmidt. He forgot about HYDRA and the pending attack. For once in his life, Steve Rogers got the girl. Reluctantly, he pulled away. He had to go. Hopefully, he'd return from this mission and ask Peggy to a dance.

After one last look at Peggy, Steve turned and jumped onto the wheel—just as the plane burst out of the tunnel. Behind him, Steve saw Phillips slam on the brakes, and he breathed a sigh of relief that they were okay. But then he looked down. The jet was flying over a huge gorge, and Steve was losing his grip. If he fell now, there was no way he would survive.

Just then, the plane's landing gear groaned and slowly started to retract. In moments, Captain America found himself inside the belly of the plane. He let out a huge breath. That had been *way* too close for comfort.

Steve's relief was short-lived. As he let go of the landing gear, he found himself looking at a huge flight deck within the belly of the giant plane. Eight fighter jets were armed and ready, their noses aimed toward the back hatch of the plane.

He'd been right! This was one of the planes that was going to attack the United States! And there were five more back inside the hangar—unless Phillips and the team had managed to stop them from taking off. Captain America had to find Red Skull—now.

Unfortunately, that was going to be a bit difficult. As he watched, the eight pilots who belonged to those fighter jets ran down from the bridge above. All of them had guns trained on Cap.

Right as the first two troopers reached him, Captain America whipped around and slammed them both with a flying spin kick. They fell to the ground, unconscious. Another one came at him, and Cap simply picked him up and threw him across the deck. He hit the far wall with a thud. The fourth trooper got smashed in the face by Captain America's shield.

Steve was holding his own—and then a huge pilot surprised him with a right hook. The punch sent Steve staggering backward onto one of the fighter jets. Inside, another pilot was sitting in the cockpit. He flicked a few switches and the jet burst to life. Another flick of the switch opened up the hatch, and before Steve could do anything, the pilot shot the plane forward—right into the open sky!

As the air whistled around him, Steve clung to the jet's hood. Slowly, he crept forward, making his way toward the cockpit. But the pilot wasn't about to let that happen. He executed a series of barrel rolls. Steve's legs flew out behind him as he struggled to hold on. Then the pilot pushed down the throttle and the plane nose-dived. Still, Steve hung on. When the plane righted itself, Steve pulled himself forward another few inches. He was within reach of the cockpit. But to get to the pilot, he'd have to punch out the glass. And that meant letting go with one hand. Steve took a deep breath. Before the pilot could make another move, he reached back his hand and then—SMASH!—he shattered the cockpit's glass, sending shards flying into the air. With one last pull, he made his way over the glass, and reaching down, released the ejector seat. Letting out a cry, the pilot was launched high into the sky.

With no one to steer it, the plane began to dive again. Climbing over the window, Captain America got into the cockpit and quickly pulled back on the throttle. When the plane was stabilized, he turned it around and flew back up, toward Red Skull's giant plane of death.

During Steve's battle with the fighter jet, Red Skull had flown the huge plane hundreds of feet away. Pressing the throttle forward as far as it could go, Steve raced after it. A hundred feet, seventy-five, fifty . . . Captain America was closing in. When he was right at the hatch, he let up on the lever and the jet flew into the bigger plane's flight deck, landing with a flash of sparks and a shriek of brakes. Finally, it came to a stop. He had made it.

Still, the fight wasn't over. Up in the cockpit, Red Skull was steering the plane closer and closer to America. And if Captain America didn't stop him, he would destroy everything and everyone Cap had been fighting for. The American Super-Soldier was battered and bruised and shaky, but he crawled out of the plane and stood up, his head held high against the evil Red Skull.

Steve had no way of knowing what was happening back at the HYDRA base. He could only hope that his team, along with Peggy and Phillips, were in control and alive. He wished that he could talk to them, find out what was going on, and tell them that it would all be okay. But he couldn't. Not yet.

Right now, he was going to get into that cockpit. And then he was going to take Schmidt down. He would figure out what was in that box Schmidt held so dear and destroy it. And then he would take the plane—and all the bombs it carried—and destroy it, too, no matter what the cost.

A year ago, Steve Rogers was just an ordinary guy hoping to join the army. Now, he was the courageous Captain America. People had given their lives to get him here, and he wouldn't let them down. Whatever the future held, he knew that he had to succeed. For Peggy and Bucky. For Erskine and Phillips. For the Howling Commandos. And most of all, for his country.

With heart, strength, and grim determination, Steve Rogers set off in the direction of the cockpit. It was time for the final confrontation. It was time for him to stop Johann Schmidt once and for all, no matter what the cost. It was time for Red Skull—and all of HYDRA—to learn that evil would never prevail over justice. Not while Captain America was there to save the day!